THE HOUSE THAT DIDN'T END

E. K. SEAVER

To request permissions, contact the author at ekseaver.author@gmail.com.

Paperback: 978-1-7374623-0-9

First paperback edition September 2021.

Edited by Angela R. Watts
Cover design © Fantastical Ink
Layout by Emily K. Seaver

Printed by IngramSpark in the USA.

Ember Ink Press
emberinkpress.wordpress.com

ekseaver.wordpress.com

For my siblings.

In castles old once stood the crown

though creeped and crumbled underground.

Lay wait in dark for fairies old

a midnight house with hor'rs untold.

Wait not for mysteries you first sought

for what you think is fully not

And nothing quite is as it seems

and black is left of the whitest queen.

The moon rests in the sky alone

Come keep and weep the heart of stone.

Worlds beneath and midnight sky

use the key to stab the eye.

When all is done and all is made

And two rot together in one grave.

Once some feel pain and others death

Will safe night darkness take a breath.

-    *E. K. Seaver*   -

1

Ly

"Stairs, oh stairs, where are you?" A young woman shoved a freckled finger onto the point of the map marking the secret door. She'd looked everywhere it had instructed, from pulling back peeling wallpaper, to digging her fingernails into the wooden floor, but the staircase was nowhere to be found. She had checked this room, and the next room over. The dust in there had made her sneeze. She tried to check upstairs but had been prevented by the boy currently sitting in front of her. "Are you going to help me or not, Joshua?"

"It's Jackson." The boy craned his neck to look over the back of the huge wingback chair. "And I'm trying to help. I'm thinking."

She tilted her head and walked over to the chair across from him, plopping into it. The fire made the room warm, but not too hot since the chill from the window behind them balanced the heat. Her phone in her back pocket buzzed, alerting her that the battery was on fifteen percent. Too bad the creepy old house didn't have electricity. Though, she figured, it wouldn't be as creepy and old if it did. She tossed the phone on the side table next to her chair and glanced at the time. It was nearly 1:00 AM. "You can think?"

If the firelight hadn't been glinting off his glasses, she would have seen him roll his eyes. "Just be quiet for a few minutes, Ly."

"I was quiet for an hour, Jeffery, and when I came back you were sleeping." The edges of the map crinkled under her tense grip. The fire crackled, sending strange shadows up the carved panels of the wall, and ashes scattering across the rug. Vermont winters required a fireplace in every home, but modern homes had precautions in place to keep the ashes from scattering. Ly drummed her fingers on the small table beside her chair. "I really need to find the stairs if I'm going to win the scavenger hunt."

"It's still Jackson. The map's been hidden in the woodwork for thirty years." The firelight flickered strangely across his jet hair and pale skin. He looked like a painting: rumbled and disgruntled but somehow perfect at the same time. "No one else is here, so I doubt you're going to have problems waiting another hour."

"A *whole* 'nother hour?" Ly's blue eyes widened and she sank back into the chair with a groan. The words started tumbling out. "I can't take this for another hour. I need to find the money so that I can start my art business so that I don't have to get a real job and I can prove to my family that you can be creative and still make money."

He nodded slowly, still watching the flames. "Then go find us some food. And maybe a blanket. It's cold."

The floorboards underneath the carpet creaked as Ly rolled out of her chair and flopped to the rug. Jackson barely glanced at her as she lay there for a few moments. Then she hopped to her feet and scampered off to find food. Of course she realized the danger of sneaking around in an ancient house in the woods. Yes, it was even more dangerous to be trapped in that house during a snowstorm with a boy she had only met four hours and six minutes ago. If the scavenger hunt wasn't offering her five-hundred dollars, she wouldn't have signed up. It was exactly the amount she needed to buy the right canvases and website domain. But if she were to be completely honest, she found it incredibly exciting. Even if the boy—what was his name? James?—did kind of remind her of a serial killer she had seen in a movie a few weeks ago.

The kitchen was a lot easier to find than the staircase. For one, there was no secret door hiding it. For another, she'd peeked in earlier while looking for the staircase. The kitchen was dim, lit only by a flickering oil lamp on the table. Ly stared at it for a moment in fascination. She'd only seen a working oil lamp in a Civil War exhibit her dad had once dragged her to when their family was visiting Maryland. The walls were decorated with floral wallpaper that probably had looked white a hundred years ago. On the wall behind the table hung an oil painting of a woman with a pointy nose.

Ly looked at the lace-covered table. Cookies, teacups of milk, and a plate of steaming-hot brownies sat on silvery-white platters painted with black roses. These hadn't been here earlier. Maybe Jackson had prepared them when she wasn't looking. Ly fingered a blonde curl. Shouldn't there be something substantial to eat as well?

"Found anything?" The boy's voice cracked as his call echoed through the house.

"Patience, Jacob." Ly snatched up the first plate. "I'm bringing it."

Balancing multiple wet paintings, a paint tray, and a cup full of stained water was a common pastime for Ly. Three plates and two milk-cups were nothing. She walked back into the fireplace room where the boy was.

He glanced up. "Why are you balancing a plate on your head?"

She shoved the teacup of milk into his hands and slid the plate on her forearm into his lap. "Here you go."

"You know," he nibbled on one of the cookies. "You could have made two trips."

"Didn't want to."

Ly watched the boy as he first stuffed one cookie, then another into his mouth. The milk disappeared through his lips, followed by a brownie. She wondered how long it had been since he'd last eaten. His cheeks were a little sunken, and his ratty sweatshirt hung from his limbs.

After gulping down the last bit of milk, he smiled. "So I figured out the staircase's location about thirty minutes ago. I just wanted food before we started."

"Really, Jaxton?" Ly twisted a curl around her finger. "I don't have time like this to waste."

"It's—never mind. And we have plenty of time to waste. With this snow, we'll probably be stuck here for another two days."

She traced a figure-eight onto the chair arm with her finger. Two days wasn't good. Two days meant that her parents would worry and she'd get another lecture about responsibility and trustworthiness. Then she'd never be allowed independence. It would also mean that they realized she stayed overnight in a house with a dark-haired, chiseled-jawline, glasses-wearing stranger. "What the heck?"

"No, I'm not kidding." He glanced at her from the corner of his eye. "And you need to hold the map up to the light for the next clue."

She tugged the map from her pocket and chucked it at him. It fluttered lightly to the floor, about a foot from his chair. Ly's stomach practiced gymnastics. Her mom would probably try to call her tonight—Ly had lied about a sleepover with a friend—but the cell service was awful this deep into the woods. How long would it take for her parents to realize she was missing?

Jackson leaned over the arm of his chair, grabbing the map, and unfolded it. Even from her spot, Ly could make out letters spiraling into unpronounceable words. But Jackson's eyes weren't on the paper, they were on her. His eyebrows knit, forming oddly deep wrinkles on his forehead.

"What?" She met his gaze with a glare.

"Do you speak Gaelic?"

"Nah, but I'm taking Spanish Two." She coughed. Spanish two was up there in her least favorite subjects—second only to math. Art should be a more prominent subject in schools, according to her. "Why?"

"Because this is in Gaelic."

"Oh." Great, so now she was going to be stuck with a hot stranger for two days *and* get nowhere with her scavenger hunt. Goodbye, five hundred dollars.

He ran a hand through his hair, a blush faintly discoloring his pale cheeks. "I mean, I can translate it for you. I was just wondering..."

"No, yeah." Now she was blushing. Why was she blushing? "Uh, speaking Gaelic is cool."

"Yes." He cleared his throat and murmured something that she didn't understand. "Okay, this first part says:

"Wait not for mysteries you first sought
For what you think is fully not."

A pause, and more mumbling.

"And nothing is ever as it seems,
For black has taken the whitest queen."

Ly's nose wrinkled. "Are you sure you translated that right? That makes no sen—"

The rumbling of the house cut her off. She gripped the arms of her chair as it slid to the right, slamming against the wall, then jerked forward. Jackson flew from his seat, tumbling onto the floor, and clutched at the rug. The table where Ly's teacup sat tumbled over, the milk mingling with the porcelain shards. As tiny slivers of glass tinkled across the floor, the fire extinguished. The rumbling stopped and icy air flattened Ly's curls against her forehead. Outside the moon was hidden by snow-filled clouds. Darkness engulfed every corner of the room.

A single torch illuminated the darkness where the fireplace had been, casting shadows over exposed bricks and peeling paint. The second torch shone just bright enough to make out the cavern. Low ceilings sloped downward, and a mismatched array of steps descended into darkness. Ly and Jackson sat in silence as two dozen torches lit the cavern, continuing to illuminate the stairs curving out of sight. Then, in sync, they stood.

In the glint of the torches, Ly studied Jackson. He'd been sitting for so long that she'd forgotten he was almost a head taller than her. His lips were tight, but the wrinkle in between his eyebrows was completely gone. She had no idea what he might be feeling. For all she knew it was boredom. Maybe random spiral staircases opened in front of him every single day. She shrugged and stepped forward, off the rug and onto the threshold of the hearth.

"Wait."

She spun around, blonde curls flying. "What, Jackfruit?"

"Wow." He quirked an eyebrow. "That's the closest to my name you've gotten."

"That's what you wanted to tell me?"

He groaned. "No, I was going to tell you it's probably booby-trapped."

"It's not going to be booby-trapped, Jello." She crossed her arms. He was being dramatic again, just like when he'd refused to let her explore upstairs. If she listened to all the people who told her not to do things, she'd never get anywhere. Booby-trap? Ridiculous.

"Well," he hesitated. "You can find that out for yourself if you want to."

Ly's footsteps made no noise as she jogged down the first five steps. Strange, she expected an echo She spun around, smugness warm in her belly. He'd been wrong. "See, Jellybean? Perfectly—"

Jackson was gone.

If anyone had been within a mile of the house, they would have heard Ly's scream. Maybe he was playing with her. Maybe he hadn't just disappeared into thin air in a span of seconds. Or he was right. What if she had triggered a boobytrap? What if he'd disappeared because of her? Jetsam wouldn't have just left her alone, right?

"JAVELIN? JASON? J-WHATEVER-YOUR-NAME-IS? WHERE ARE YOU?"

Much to her chagrin, he didn't answer.

So he probably was stuck in the boobytrap somewhere. Well, it would take a while to find him and free him. She ignored the guilty panic settling in her chest. If she was going to try to find him, she might as well try to win her scavenger hunt, too. Maybe she'd paint a landscape of the house afterward as a memory of this event. Maybe it would sell for a thousand dollars. She traced a figure-eight into her palms. Everything was going to be alright. And because the clue had opened up the staircase, the next clue ought to be at the bottom of it.

So, she continued down the staircase, praying that each step wouldn't be her last.

2

Jackson

Powers of foresight weren't required for Jackson to know what was going to happen the moment he told Ly not to descend the staircase. Come to think of it, he couldn't remember a single time when he had told someone not to do something, and they had actually listened to him. As usual, he was fully aware he'd reap her consequences.

She snorted. "It's not going to be booby-trapped, Jello."

She knew his name. He knew she knew his name. So why did she have to be incorrigible and use every other J-word in the English language to substitute for his real name? And why was it strangely adorable and made his heart beat a little faster? He needed to be careful, or else he might fall for her. It was literally in his blood to fall in love quickly. He rolled his eyes, both at his feelings and her stubbornness. "Well, you can find that out for yourself if you want to."

He regretted the words the moment he plunged into the darkness below him. The ground tilted, forcing him backward. He grunted as his back hit the floor and suddenly he was slipping, plummeting downwards, deeper into the abyss. *Wonderful*, a slide.

There had been a playground near his home when he was younger. Once his mother had attempted to coax him down the slide. He had ended up with a bloody nose and tears all around. Maybe he'd leave this part out in the debrief to his mother later. *Hades*, he missed her. How long had it been since he'd seen her? Three months, maybe?

This slide continued its sharp drop. Jackson stared into the darkness and listened to the ominous clunking. Maybe this was how it would end—Maybe the pretty girl who just happened to stumble upon the house had been sent by the gwyllion. Maybe he'd fallen, quite literally, into their trap and maybe this was how he was going to die.

Of course, this wasn't the worst possible way to die. Falling to one's death, though not as honorable as being murdered while fighting a fiery beast, still made the list of brave deaths. Unless, of course, bleeding out was ruled to be the cause of death, and somehow gave the fae the right to extract your blood from wherever it had spilled and return it to your body. He'd complained to his mother many times about the pain of such an experience.

Actually, he didn't want to die. The mere chance that he could be revived wasn't worth the risk. So he reached out both hands to slow his slide. His one problem, he found, was that his hands were tightly bound. He wasn't quite sure how that happened, but the meta dug deeper into his skin the more he struggled. The breeze whipped his dark hair back as the slide dropped sharply.

He yelped as the floor dropped out from under him and he slammed into the seat of a chair. Cold metal locked around his wrists and ankles, and the beginnings of a headache pulsed behind his eyes. His glasses were slightly askew. Still, by the light of a pale candle, he could see the room. The silver chair securing his wrists glinted in the flame. He shifted in the seat as the cold metal shackles chafed at his wrist. At least the fae had been right about this house being filled with dark magic.

Surely the humans could feel it, too. They'd probably call it haunted. And yet for some reason, they sent Ly on a scavenger hunt to come here. Unless, of course, she was a gwyllion trap. He pushed the thought away.

But who in bloody hades would send children traipsing around a haunted house?

Besides the fae, of course. He couldn't be more than two years older than Ly, but the fairies had sent him to destroy their evil counterparts.

A metal band emerged from the chair and tightened around his chest his chest, pushing the dagger hidden under his sweatshirt against his ribcage. "Blast."

With that word, the dim candle at the center of the room flickered out. He sucked in a breath. Why couldn't he have grabbed his sword? Instead, it sat useless in the umbrella stand beside the door, because Ly disliked it. He should have kept it on him. Not that he could use it much, with his hands chained. Still, he was better with a sword than a dagger.

It took him an embarrassingly long time to notice the pale smoke, glimmering like a nearly dead glow-stick. It came from the corner of the room, creeping across the floor in an unhurried roll. Fear rarely made its way into his gut, but it weaseled in this time. The smoke burned with an icy breath as it brushed his bare feet. He stared at his pale toes. Where in the world had his shoes gone?

The smoke rose, wafting the ceiling and back down again, burning every time it brushed his skin and leaving red welts in its wake. Finally, the smoke billowed into two columns a few feet away from his chair. One took the shape of a beautiful woman, so intricately crafted in the smoke that her hair almost took on its natural shade of auburn. *Elvira.* His mother. The other column morphed into another woman, her dress long and silky green. A gwyllion. The gwyllion's shape rushed into Elvira. Blood—not smoke—poured from the fairy queen's neck.

Then the picture was gone.

Jackson swallowed the panic. It couldn't be true. It was his fears, his imagination. The fairy queen wasn't dead—there was no way she could have been killed by a common gwyllion. He ignored the nausea in his stomach. No, he wouldn't believe it.

The smoke moved again.

It formed into a box, with one side open towards him, allowing him to see into it. A Ly-shaped figure was locked inside, her body fashioned from translucent swirling smoke. She pressed on the walls, beating them, pushing them as they moved inwards. She hunched over as the roof lowered. Her mouth opened in a mute scream. Jackson's eyes drifted to her hands, where thick shackles crushed her wrists. Pain was etched where there had earlier been stupidity and snark. Tears—real tears—trickled down smoky cheeks.

Her form sat down on the floor of the box as it closed in. It paused from its crushing movements as she stared at the glinting chains on her wrists. She trembled with sobs, shaking her head back and forth. Her hair slipped out of its ponytail, curling gently around her face.

Jackson struggled at his bonds. He wouldn't let them do this to her. The gwyllion could attack him, that was fine. He already had scars proving that they weren't above it. Pulling a mortal woman—practically still a child—into the conflict crossed a line; regardless of how annoying that girl was. The arms of his chair grew gold shackles, locking his wrists and feet in place. He tried to slide his hand out from the shackle, but it tightened. No, he couldn't let the evil fae do this. By no means was this fighting fair. She didn't deserve this.

The smoke box moved again. Ly pulled her knees closer to her and ducked her head. The box pressed inward, squeezing, squeezing, squeezing. She moved her body into a strange contortion. Jackson tried to lean forward, willing it to stop. They couldn't have gotten to her this fast. This image was impossible, right? *Right?* A metal band formed across his chest, holding him back. He didn't even notice the trail of tears on his cheeks. "No, no. Stop. Please."

The box shrunk. Something cracked. Her scream pierced through the smoke. Blonde hair hung around a broken neck. Her smoke-formed flesh shriveled and fell from her face until all remaining was a yellowed skeleton.

Jackson leaped up, the bonds melting from his body like butter. The smoke vanished, plunging the room into utter darkness. And then the floor dropped out from under him. Again.

3

Ly

The only time Ly liked being alone was when she had eighties music on and was painting in her room. The creaking of an old building most certainly wasn't eighties and said old building wasn't her room. And the cracking sea-green walls were probably painted in the eighties— eighteen-eighties, that was.

And she was alone.

For the third time in the last hour, she felt panic grip her chest. She needed to find the end of the scavenger hunt and then find Jackson. Get the money, save the boy. Start a successful art business and live happily ever after. The to-do list didn't include three mild panic attacks.

She glared down yet another set of three doors. About three rooms ago, she'd gotten the feeling that there was something more to this booby-trapped house than just being old. It gave her a creepy feeling like she'd gotten while reading about villains in fairy tales as a child. But magic was just in stories and this house was very real. She peered at the ceiling far above. Gold embellishments glittered in the electric lamps that somehow worked in the basement. This did seem like a rather odd place to hide notes for a scavenger hunt. Uncertainty pounded at her heart. What if this wasn't the right house? What if the clue in Schiller's Oak had been talking about something else?

She had found the ancient-looking paper leading her here in a knot in the tree. She was at least two clues ahead of everyone else when she found it and the snow began to fall. It had read something like:

"In castles old once stood the crown
Though creeped and crumbled underground
Something-something fairies old
Something-house-something untold"

Was there another old mansion in Stowington? Even after living nearby her whole life, she hadn't heard of any older buildings. She studied the three doors in front of her. The blue one to the left glistened in the light like the paint was fresh. A metal grate covered the middle door, casting shadows onto its rusted red exterior. On the right, however, a bright yellow one sat with a sun-shaped mirror in its center.

She traced a figure-eight into the palm of her hand, repeating the motion several times. She took a deep breath and her stomach growled loud enough to echo through the tall hallway. Would the house provide more magical food for her? Cookies and brownies weren't exactly enough to substitute for a lost lunch and dinner. And breakfast, maybe. She'd been down here a long time.

She tugged on a golden curl and laughed to herself. Food magically popping up was about as likely as Jamboree making an observation without topping it off with a sarcastic comment; ergo, impossible.

The wind whistled through an unseen crack, sending an eruption of goosebumps down Ly's arms. One of the two lightbulbs flickered, then went out. Ly traced her eights again and again as the cold darkness crept around. She was alone. Completely and utterly alone. No sane person in the twenty-first century could completely ignore the thoughts creeping into her head in the deepest of darknesses, in a strange house all alone.

In this matter, Ly was perfectly sane. She reminded herself to breathe, breathe, *breathe*. What if Jackson had lured her here just too— No, she couldn't think that. It wasn't true. He was a perfectly fine person who was possibly in danger and needed her help. She forced the nauseating thoughts from her mind. Right now, her priority was to save him.

The yellow door's handle chilled her fingers, and she pressed her whole body against it to get it to budge just wide enough for her small frame to enter. She slipped through, moving into the room when she felt something tug on the corner of her sweater. She gasped and spun around to face the ferocious door handle upon which her sweater had snagged. With an annoyed sigh, she pulled the fabric off of the handle and turned to survey the room.

It was almost blindingly bright, with the entire walls and spiraling stairs glowing white. Stairs? She blinked again at what looked like the optical illusions her mom used to paint. A flight of stairs ascended to one level, descended to the next, and flipped upside down at the third. It looked like a giant puzzle-maze of never ending stairs. Her calves burned. It reminded her like the stairs at a waterpark—she just hoped what was at the end would be more satisfying than a twelve-second-long waterslide.

Needless to say, Ly didn't like waterparks.

Still, there came a time in a person's life where they must climb higher than they thought they could to succeed, and Ly knew this was her moment. So she started up the stairs, taking them two at a time.

At stair thirteen came the first direction change. She jogged down a few stairs, then up to her right. Up a little further, then to the left. Another dozen steps and she decided to start taking them one at a time. Her calves ached after step forty-seven. At step forty-eight, her left calf seized up and refused to support her weight.

She lowered herself to the step and pulled up the leg of her jeans. The bright lighting of the room made her skin look vampire-pale. She pressed her fingers against her calf and massaged the aching muscles. "Good gobsmackers."

Cursing in candy was simply the only way to express the excruciating amounts of pain in her legs. She looked up. How many steps were left in this maze?

No ceiling was detectable, only layers upon layer of more stairs rising above. Her stomach growled. Speaking of candy, she was still hungry. And the only way to get candy was to find the end of the stairs and rescue Jackson and get out of the house.

She laid back against the stairs, running her hands through her curls. Okay, she needed to get up now. She rolled onto her stomach. The edge of one of the steps pushed into her cheek. She pushed herself onto all fours and climbed, stair by stair, to the next platform.

While the other seven platforms had turned directly onto a single staircase, this one divided into two—one running up, and the other down. She plopped, criss-cross-applesauce in the middle of the square platform. She peered over the side. Stairs twisted like snakes below her, intertwined in a confusing maze of white and shadows.

She could go down, but down was where she'd started. So she turned, and ignoring her cramping muscles, forced herself to her feet and climbed up the flight of the stairs leading up. The platform turned again at the top of the stairs, and she turned with it. *Step, step, step.* She yawned. How much farther? And what time was it? She reached for her phone in her back pocket but felt nothing.

"Gosh-darn Doritos." In her mind's eye, she saw herself set it on the small table beside her chair, a dozen rooms ago when Jackson's existence was still confirmable. Where was he now? What if he had fallen into a pit of spiders? Or worse, bumblebees? What if someone. . . She turned around and looked out, yet again, over the expanse of stairs.

That's about the point where she noticed that the golden cloud of hair normally cascading over her shoulders was hanging—up? The back part of her shirt that wasn't tucked in left a cold and exposed piece of skin on her back. Her mind only took a few seconds to make the gravitational shift and realize that she was hanging upside down.

She screamed.

The house, in all of its intricacies, must have interpreted her scream as a request to leave the stairs, because in the span of a blink, Ly no longer hung from the stairs. Instead, dim candlelight flickered across shelves of books. And for the first time in at least eight years, Ly found herself in a library.

A library was nearly as bad as an upside-down staircase. Libraries meant studying and school and useless knowledge. Ly frowned at the floor-to-ceiling rows of books. Jeopardy probably liked libraries. Maybe, for some strange reason, the house, with all of its strange abilities, had dumped him here.

She pushed herself to her feet and stared at the ceiling. Magic wasn't real, so how on earth had she fallen through the roof unharmed? After a moment's contemplation, she decided she had popped through a trapdoor like the one Jump-rope had fallen through. Either way, she might as well go find him.

It took about four rows for frustration to growl in the pit of her stomach. *She* was trying to find him. The least he could do is make a little effort to be found. Another dozen rows and she slowed her pace. On the next row, she stopped, leaned against the bookcase, and slid to the ground. Tears burned behind her eyelids. What if he wasn't there, because he had left when she turned her back? She barely knew him; there was no reason for him to stay.

Still, somewhere deep inside her, she had hoped that he would help her. But now she was lost and all alone in an old house that was probably haunted. She shook her head, begging the tears not to come, but they slipped out of her eyes anyways.

She closed her eyes, letting herself feel the anger and fear and sadness balled up inside of her, letting the tears become their own sort of waterfall and wet her cheeks, cascading down her neck and soaking her shirt.

She wasn't sure how long she'd been crying, but a dull headache throbbed at the back of her neck when she opened her eyes again. She stared at the row of books across from her, zoning out for a moment on the dark leather spines.

And then her eyes came back into focus. Something was out of place—a little corner of paper sticking out from between two covers. Using the bookcase behind her for support, she stood. Everything blurred, then focused. She snatched the corner of the paper. It was the same paper as the clues had been, but this time with metallic font.

The letters sharpened before her eyes

"The moon rests in the sky alone
Come and keep the heart of stone
Worlds beneath and midnight sky
Use the key to stab the eye."

She blinked, and then reread it. Ew, she needed to stab someone's eye? Whose? She murmured the words of the clue over and over again. A little prick in her chest said that she would find Jackson at the end of the clues. And right now, she cared more about finding him than finding her money.

4

Jackson

Beads of sweat ran down Jackson's face and mingled in the boiling water surrounding him. The steam fogged his glasses. The burning liquid raised thick, puss-filled welts across his arms and neck. His bottom lip was numb as another welt grew on it, the tingling crawling as the swelling temporarily deadened the agony. Searing pain rippled through his body and shocks of dizziness stirred his mind, but if he slouched the slightest bit, his nose would submerge. He wouldn't be able to breathe. His jaw clenched. His senses begged for him to sleep, but succumbing to the dark spots speckling his vision meant drowning.

For the first time in months, his magic flared with his anger, shooting electric sparks from his exposed skin. He grimaced. Whoever had engineered this torture was genius. The metal cuffs around his ankles, attached to the bottom of the pot, scorched his skin. He fiddled with the rope around his hands, glaring at the water around him. The ropes chafed at the burns and the bubbling pink flesh.

His glasses slid off his nose, plonking into the water.

Hades, even if he did escape now, visibility would be extremely limited. Only magical things could be seen clearly without his glasses. Terror gripped his chest, matching the pain with its intensity. It'd be nearly impossible to find Ly—he wouldn't even be able to see her if her body was lying six feet in front of him. If she wasn't dead yet, both of them would probably die in this never-ending maze. He shifted his weight, wishing the liquid would make him more buoyant, wishing the cauldron he stood in weren't so tall and slick. Burning welts bubbled along his arms as he stood hoping, hoping that the image of Ly he had seen in the smoke was simply a figment of his imagination and not what was actually happening to her.

Then something snapped—the rope around his hands, to be specific. It slithered, snake-like from his hands to the pot's floor as the water's temperature dropped. The rope brushed against his feet as the shackles unlatched and sunk to the bottom of the pot. Was there a djinn nearby, granting wishes? The icy water soothed his burned skin, mixing with the fae blood and healing the smaller of his wounds. He closed his eyes and dunked himself all the way underwater, reveling in the coolness.

When he came back up again, the pain dispersed into chill bumps, although the worry in his stomach still sent bile into the back of his throat. The water had receded to below his chin. He grabbed the edge of the pot, but jerked away as the blister in the center of his palm stung. He plunged it into the icy water and sat in silence. If he could push through the pain and escape—

One of the shadows moved—that, or his eyes were tricking him. But no, there it was again, moving in the darkness. And, after a moment, it glowed.

Oh, hades. He backed up against the pot, as far away from the figure as possible. This was not good. He planned to get in, get the Moonlock necklace, and get out. He hadn't wanted— No, this was bad. He felt for the dagger at his side. *Still there.* But she wasn't close enough.

Her features sharpened like someone was adjusting binocular lenses. Pale skin, high cheekbones. Narrow green eyes with a psychotic amusement. Nose and chin sharp enough to cut through diamonds, and a mouth perpetually puckered into a smirk. Her midnight hair was the most human of her features, hanging lush and shining around her thin face.

And she wore the emerald robes of a gwyllion.

Jackson gripped his dagger tighter as his breath billowed out in puffs in the suddenly freezing room. For once, he wished he had practiced magic rather than stealth fighting. His metal would be no match for her powers, and she probably was the one protecting the locket. "What do you want?"

"What a harsh way to greet family, Jackson." Her voice was like a psychopathic harp. "It's been such a long time. You've grown up so handsomely. I take it the fae have treated you well when they're not sending you on dangerous quests?"

"Something like that." He grimaced. "What do you want with me?"

Her eyebrows tilted upward as if she was offended that he would ask. "You came to my threshold. It was only polite for me to let you in."

Not for the first time in his life did Jackson wish that he wasn't half-fae. Then he wouldn't have to see her wretched smile when his glasses were off. He raised himself on tip-toe so she wasn't peering down at him so demeaningly. He opened his mouth to retort, but the woman cut him off.

"Oh dear, my cousin. The human in you burns easily, doesn't it?"

He thought of the scalding sunburns he had received on one of his quests through Alabama. "You don't know half of it."

"*Half*," She chuckled. "Funny."

"Uh... yeah."

"So, cousin, have you got a fiancée yet? I've heard in fae culture they marry young. And you're, what, nineteen?"

"Eighteen." This conversation was not going the way he'd expected it to.

"Ah yes, of course." She paced around the room, her green skirts moving almost river-like around her legs. If Jackson could leap from the pot—how difficult would it be to jump from behind and stab her?

"And you are?"

"Twenty-two. Young to be a guardian, yet there are so few of us living to old age." She sighed, turning back around and brushing a dark lock behind her pointed ear. "Our kind, dear cousin would survive much longer if we had richer meat."

"You have the forest animals." Jackson couldn't keep the bitterness from his tongue. "You don't need humans."

She clicked her tongue. "No need for anger, cousin. You're practically a light fae now, having been raised by them. I should not assume you'd understand our struggles."

"Your struggles will end the human race." He glared at her.

"Enough about my problems. You didn't answer my question. Is there any girl in your life? Any at all?"

"Why do you ask?" Jackson felt the heat of a blush crawl up his neck. Why had his first thought been of Ly?

"Why do you avoid the question?"

"Because I don't have an answer."

"Very well, then." She smiled the beaming smile that she, like all the vampire-esque gwyllion, used to lure men in before killing them and feasting on their flesh. "Anyways, cousin, I heard you were in town and I just knew you had to drop in for a while."

"Drop in. Heh." Jackson attempted to avoid looking at his cousin's face. "Very funny. Maybe next time you shouldn't leave me in boiling water for two hours."

She grinned again, her fangs curved and sharp in the glistening light. "Cousin, you exaggerate. I left you close to twenty minutes to ensure you were well done. You're the closest thing to human flesh nearby in a long time. The hunters are gone searching, but our feast has come anyway if you refuse to join us."

Ah, here was the inevitable sales pitch. Fine, he would humor her. "Assist you?"

She snorted. "You know your mother, may she rest in fury, was never allowed to leave the forests. Your halfling blood grants you privileges beyond fathom. Can't you imagine what it must be like in our shoes? Us, your gwyllion kin, confined to the forests because of that awful Moonlock. I know you have the key, Jackson. All you have to do is unlock the locket, and we'll be free."

"Free to slaughter humanity."

"Well, you oughtn't to phrase it as such." She shook her head, long hair rippling. "We are bound to the forest, eternally locked in this cage, forbidden on paths where humans walk. We must be free to live, and you hold the key to our survival. If only you could provide the key, we shall survive. One species for another, is that not fair?"

"Very eloquent." Jackson rolled his shoulders. One of the welts on his back burst, sending a shock of pain through his body. Wisps of red drifted through the water. "I'm not joining you."

Hecate's nostrils flared, and she smirked. "There are other ways of getting it, cousin."

She snapped her fingers, and suddenly the boiling water and the pot vanished, and Jackson found himself standing, soaked, with glasses returned to the bridge of his nose. He pushed them up and scanned the room. Bones lay around the edges, a few human skulls littered the floor. Metal objects—knives, chain mail, forks—mingled with the remains. Jackson avoided his cousin's gaze even while her glare penetrated him.

She sighed, finally, recapturing his attention. "I killed her if you must know."

Jackson's pain showed before he could mask it. "Thought so."

"It was shockingly uneventful. I thought she would fight to survive."

"She preferred peace." *She preferred sending her adopted children on dangerous quests to save the fae.* He stared at the ground. He wasn't even sure who he was angry at—Hecate for murdering his mother or his mother for sending him away the moment he came of age. Fierce electricity pulsed through his veins, begging to surface, begging to kill. The curse of the male gwyllion— their power was angry and deadly.

"You cannot be peaceful if you cannot be violent." The harp-like lilt morphed to staccato cello notes. "To refuse to defend yourself when you are the lifeblood of a race is weakness."

The electricity sent static through Jackson's body. He wanted to scream at his cousin. Queen Elvira wasn't weak. She hadn't wanted to hurt anyone. She was willing to sacrifice everything to protect her people. Jackson met the gwyllion's eyes with a steady gaze, trying to hide glassy eyes.

"Awww," Hecate smirked. "Is Jackson going to cry?"

The power surged out from him too fast, sending unstoppable coils of electricity crackling from his body. The sharp odor of burnt flesh filled his nose. No, it wasn't supposed to be like this. He could control it—but he hadn't. The streaks radiated across the room, furious and burning. The use of his power soothed the pussy wounds on his flesh. Glossy smoke poured through the room. Hecate was gone. Through the hazy silver smoke, he saw a door, an escape from the potential harm both being caused by and being done to him. Without a second thought, he sprinted through it, undeterred by the soaking clothes sloshing against his body.

5

Ly

Ly flopped down on a conveniently placed couch. There were no keys and no eyes and she was stuck in a giant library with no way out. She had checked three times. Jackson was nowhere in the library and it had to be at least two A.M. She stared at the paper in her hands for the five-hundredth time. What could she be missing?

Moon, sky, the heart of stone. She glanced around her. There were no stone heart statues, biologically accurate or otherwise. She'd seen moons on some of the spines, but nothing with hearts or eyes. Only one book was by someone with the last name Heart was a cookbook she'd turned inside out. Or perhaps "eye" referred to the "I" section of the library. Could she find a key there that would allow her to stab something? That made far more sense than blinding someone for no good reason. But her legs hurt and her eyes hurt and she kind of wanted to rest rather than searching for eye-keys and mysterious boys who disappeared into trapdoors.

So she closed her eyes for a few minutes, letting all of the thoughts drift from her head. All of the thoughts except for the nagging feeling that she did need to get up and find Jackson and save him. She had enough of that feeling after approximately forty-seven seconds, and she stood, throwing her legs over the front of the couch and jumping to her feet.

Find the eye—erm, the "i"s

The rows felt longer than they had been a little while ago. *A, B, C, D, E, F...* She trailed off with her humming. She was seventeen, for goodness's sake. She ought to know how far along 'I' was in the alphabet. *G,* she read the authors' names.

Gudge, Persephone
Gukflak, Exerstien
Gyoup, Hisendal

She didn't recognize any of the names. Not that she read very much. Were these books even in English? The titles didn't look like discernible words to her. She moved three aisles down, but the 'G's continued. *Gladshaw, Gufnyd...* Another three aisles and she reached the 'H's, and four more for the 'I's She stopped on the first row of 'I's. Was she going to have to scan all of these books to find a single book that may or may not even hold the answer to the riddle that she was looking for? And what if she had missed something? What if this wasn't even the order of the riddles that she was supposed to be in?

Iduna, E. A.
Iigret, Nathalia
Ise, Key

Key. Ly stared at the book for a moment before fingering the leathered spine. There was no clue peeking out from underneath the book, so it must be inside. She jerked the book from its resting place on the shelf.

As someone who didn't read, Ly's imagination was filled more with nature scenes and beautiful landscapes than with hidden doors and secret passageways, which is why she jumped back and hit her elbow when a portion of the shelf swung inwards. Stairs descended sharply and dust floated out into the dim light of the library. If the last secret passageway had taken Jefferson from her, then this one might bring him back.

A light shone somewhere at the bottom of the stairs—the ceiling dropped too sharply for Ly to see—and the steps were a little bit slippery as if someone had barely tried to wipe spilled oil off of the stairs. The walls were made of jagged stone that cut into Ly's palms as she clung to them in her descent. As she exited the passageway, a door slammed behind her.

The room was large and circular, dimly lit by a luminescent puddle of water in the middle of the floor. Every odd and end imaginable lay scattered about. What was this place? It looked like a fantasy drawing from an adult coloring book for grownups who liked to use gloomy colors and dwell on broken objects and dead bodies.

Bodies. She made out the shape of bones intermingled with the broken objects, and a figure lying motionless across the room. Ly's heart leaped into her throat and she rushed across the room, kneeling beside the woman.

The figure was young, maybe a couple of years older than Ly, with pale skin and a snobbishly pointed nose. Ly stared. Not only did this room look like a fantasy picture, but this woman did too. Something like a grown-up Snow White from the Grimm's fairy tales, with ebony hair and scarlet lips, her long Hampshire-green renaissance-styled dress splayed around her.

Ly touched the woman's shoulder. Was she allowed to do this? Was it okay to randomly touch dead people's shoulders? "Are you alive?"

The woman groaned and rolled over. Ly blinked. She could have sworn that the woman's skin was glowing the faintest pale, illuminating the room just enough to see. The lady's long, black hair shimmered in her glow, and angular green eyes fluttered open, staring back at Ly's blue ones.

The woman's lips parted. Her voice was honey-soft, yet it struck the chord of danger to a near-forgotten instinct in Ly. "Hello there, who are you?"

"I'm Ly." She brushed a golden curl behind her ear. "I'm on a scavenger hunt and I found this other guy who was going to help me but then he disappeared and I got lost and was scared—are you okay, though?"

The woman pushed herself into a sitting position, making her taller than a squatting Ly. Her hair rippled down her back, and Ly couldn't help but stare. The woman's locks let off the same unearthly glow. The corners of her lips curved into a graceful smile. "Yes, I think I'm better now. You may call me Hecate."

Ly stood up and offered her hand to Hecate, who accepted it and pulled herself to her feet. "I'm glad you're okay."

The woman was tall—at least a head taller than Ly. The two stood in awkward silence. The bioluminescent water cast strange shadows across the room. After a moment Hecate snapped her fingers. Two torches flared opposite each other in the circular room. Ly's mouth dropped open. Hecate chuckled and tucked a strand of dark hair behind her ear. "You've never seen magic before, have you, love?"

"Magic isn't real." Ly shook her head, awe frozen on her features. At least, she'd always thought it wasn't, but whatever Hecate had just done sure looked like real magic. "How did you do it?"

"Well, I had a remote in my hand, and when I pressed this button..." The woman opened her palm. Nothing was there.

"Uhm..." Ly's eyebrows knitted. What in the world was happening? Who was this lady? And was her magic the real, wish-upon-a-star kind? That was impossible, right?

Amusement wrinkled around Hecate's eyes. "I'm teasing. I want nothing to do with mortal devices, love. I prefer magic. Pure fae magic."

Ly nodded like she understood. She didn't. "Okay. So what happened to you? Why were you on the ground?"

"That's quite a long story, love."

"I have time."

"It was my cousin." Hecate's gaze drifted to the ground, but not before Ly saw tears form in her emerald eyes. "He came here searching for an object, the Moonlock, to destroy our people."

"Why?"

"Because he cares nothing for us. He is angry that his mother died and his father abandoned him, and he was taken in by our enemies. He believes that he must kill us for his father's people to be safe."

Ly scratched her nose. It was kinda stuffy down here. "Wouldn't killing all of you, all of his mom's people, kill him too?"

Hecate shook her head. "He is half-human. He would be sick for a very long time after he destroys it, but he would live. I sought the key that he holds—if we had the key, we would be freed from the forest and allowed to roam. It is because of my cousin that his kin are locked inside the darkest parts of the wood."

Ly's legs hurt. She looked around, but she couldn't find a chair. "That's awful."

"It is." Hecate sighed. "I remember when he was born—I was nigh four years old. He was hope for our kind—a bridge between the human and fae worlds. But when his mother died and the enemy fae took him in, they raised him to hate us. He believes that we are in the wrong. Jackson has spent his whole life trying to kill us."

"Who?" Ly blinked. Jacoby? Really? But he seemed so— nice wasn't the right word. Kind, maybe? Not like a genocidal maniac.

"Jackson. My cousin." Hecate's eyes grew wide, and without warning, she swept Ly into an embrace. "Oh, dear child, please tell me you have not stumbled across him in your time here."

"Uh..." Ly squeaked. The hug was almost painfully tight. "I have. He didn't seem bad."

"Of course he didn't. Nothing is as it seems." Hecate released the tongue-tied girl. "You poor thing, I'm so glad you're alive."

Ly was going to say something like "thank you" or "me too," but it came out as "Me you." She blushed.

Hecate ignored her blunder, instead pacing the room as Ly watched. Suddenly Hecate whipped around, her long hair rippling. "Does Jackson trust you?"

Ly shrugged. "Maybe?"

"If he trusts you, there may be a way to save my kind. Would you help me with that?"

Ly hesitated. Maybe Juniper was bad. Maybe helping Hecate was the best idea. But he'd been kind to her, and he was sweet and a little silly and kind of handsome. She stared at the floor. Handsome didn't mean good. He might have been lying to her. And he wanted to destroy an entire race, so he kind of had to be bad, right?

"Yeah." She nodded. "I'll help if you want me to."

Hecate pulled back one of the draperies of her robe and withdrew a necklace—a complex full moon on a thin silver chain. It had to be the most beautiful necklace Ly had ever seen, glinting as it spun around on the twisted chain. "This is the Moonlock. Will you put this on, love? Do not let him see it, nor touch it. He won't suspect you're wearing it, and it will protect you from any harm he attempts."

Hecate passed over the necklace. Ly held it in her palm, running her fingers over the detailed designs. Layers of thin glass and metal swirled in a circle, forming little divots to represent the craters of the moon. In the center rested a tiny keyhole. It made Ly want to paint a moonscape. Maybe a summery scene with sand and rolling ocean waves. She unclasped the chain, draping the necklace over her shoulders, then refastened it.

And then everything went black.

6

Jackson

Jackson really hated running. It wasn't that the running itself was a problem—he did enjoy the feeling of the wind rushing through his hair and the pounding of the ground underneath his feet. He just didn't enjoy panicked running, least of all in a humid castle that seemed to go on forever.

He kept running though, forcing his mind to focus on Ly and not the sweat dripping down his forehead. It was uncomfortable to feel so attached to her, and he didn't know why he developed, what was the word—a crush—on her. Maybe she reminded him of someone in memory long suppressed. What Jackson did know though, was Ly's life was in danger. Who knew what his cousin had done to her. The pictures in the smoke had made it clear that the gwyllion knew about her, but Hecate hadn't tried to use the girl as a bargaining tool. That meant that Ly was out of the gwyllions' grasp.

Either out of their grasp or dead.

He didn't want to think about the latter option.

Although his fae blood, combined with Hecate's powers, almost eliminated his boils, sore spots still ached around his skin. He slowed his pace to a jog. Could it hurt Ly for him to slow down? Saving strength was a good thing. He glanced over his shoulder at the curving hallway behind him. *Hades*, he could have sworn that he was walking in circles, but he hadn't stumbled upon the x that he'd scratched into the stone wall, so maybe he was changing directions. Or perhaps the floor sloped enough that he was underneath the place he had just walked. A tendril of tension wound through his gut. What if he was just getting farther from Ly? What if she ended up dead because of it? What if she was already dead?

The thoughts seeped into his head. He shouldn't let them get to him—he knew they were just an accessory of the house. Maybe they were creeping into his head because Elvira was gone. Pain twisted his stomach, and he pushed back the tears. His mother—adopted mother—was someone he'd gone to the ends of the earth for on numerous occasions. She'd always been there for him, even while he was off on quests. And he'd nearly always been there to protect her. But he hadn't been when...

The darkness all around him crept inside. Not even fae blood could stop one's heart from breaking. Thin fog swirled through the corridor. Anxiety seized Jackson's heart. No, no, he couldn't do this again. No more smoke pictures. He couldn't stand to see those he loved die. He turned around to flee back up the hallway. There had to be some other way to find her, without suffering through these images.

But the passage behind him was shut, sealed with a thick stone wall just like those around him. There was no escape from the smoke as it increased, billowing up into figures and vague memories. He closed his eyes and backed up until he felt the stone against the wall. He couldn't do this now. Ever. He couldn't see them die again. He struggled to force air into his lungs.

Cold fingers brushed across his cheek. He opened his eyes. It took a moment for them to focus on the smokey form in front of him. Elvira. His mother.

That's when the tears broke loose. She was gone. His mother was gone. He hunched over, the pain in his gut overwhelming, sickening. He hadn't been able to protect her. He should have been there. He looked up, the feel of his mother's touch lingering on his cheek. Her smoke form was gone, too, although the vapor still covered the floor and formed old memories, thin and insubstantial. The tears erased their already blurry forms.

He didn't know how long he sat there, the pale glow of the smoke the only thing to light the dark hallway. After hours— maybe two or three, he stood. His mother was gone. It felt like his head was underwater. Emotions flooded him, receded, and rushed back in. He couldn't change that his mother was gone. He couldn't change that he wasn't there to protect her, but he could save Ly. That was what his mother would have wanted him to do. She wouldn't have wanted him to grieve, not when someone else needed saving.

He had been sent to destroy something and save the world, but now he fully accepted his responsibility to save someone. Just a single person who suddenly was more important than the entire world to him. And he would make sure she left the house alive.

A bare spark of confidence burned in him. He would save Ly. For his mother.

Smoke drifted lazily around his feet, yet each step felt heavy. He blocked out the dark, terrifying thoughts and focused on finding her. Hecate couldn't kill Ly too. He would rescue the innocent girl. He needed to do it for his mother. He needed to do it for himself.

He ran again. The wet clothes continued to chafe his skin, but still he ran. Darkness swam around him as the walls of the underground maze shifted and spun, leaving him no way to backtrack and a dozen paths forward. Footfalls echoed everywhere. In front, behind, above—anywhere but below him. The noise begged him to slow down, to watch over his shoulder. It insisted there was something to be afraid of following him, and a terrible nightmare ahead of which to beware. *Turn around, turn around*, the slithering words crept into his ears. *You're in danger.*

"I know." He panted the words.

Turn back now, the voice morphed from a terrifying whisper into words—loud, audible words—yet still inside his head. Hecate's voice whispered to him. *And I promise you won't be hurt.*

Breaths came more difficult through the smoke-filled chambers, but he pushed forward, speaking into the dark. "You'll hurt Ly."

Why do you care? She is nothing to you.

Except she wasn't. She was much more than nothing. She was all the semblance of reason that he had left. Ly needed him. He needed her. Something inside him lurched at the thought.

He didn't like needing people. The only person he had needed before was his mother. But now she was gone. Because of Hecate.

"I do care. You can't have her."

Eheheh.

What did that mean? Jackson stumbled forward, his ankle twisting under him. No! No, Hecate couldn't have her. His insides twisted. He slowed, then stopped. "No."

His words echoed emptily in the darkness.

He yelled, "You can't have her!"

There was no response.

He sprinted forward, pushing himself to run as fast as he could. No, no, Hecate couldn't hurt Ly. Not someone else. Pain shot through his leg, but he pushed through the stabbing hurt.

He was going to find Ly. He was going to save her.

You're going the wrong way, Cousin.

Jackson slowed, then came to a panting stop. "You're kidding."

No, it was just fun to watch you run. You're utterly awful at it, you know. I've never seen such bad form in my life.

"You've never been outside the forest."

The cavern groaned like it was tired of standing, her response to his taunts.

He panted, trying to catch his breath. "Are you lying to me?"

Do I lie to you, Cousin?

"Yes."

She is behind you. I swear on the gwyllion.

He murmured a thanks and spun around. The wall perpetually closing in behind him had morphed into a staircase, rising so high he barely made out the midnight black door at the top.

As quickly as it had appeared, the smoke drained away, leaving the staircase lit only by a dull light leaking out from the cracks at the edge of the door. He had no choice but to scale the steps in the dark. He climbed, forcing himself up stair after stair, partially tempted to count them, but too tired to execute the action. Fifty-or-so steps up, the top still rested high above him. If Ly wasn't here, this was a total waste of time. But Hecate had sworn on her people that Jackson would find the girl at the top of the stairs. His toes throbbed from being scuffed against the stones, and his eyes hurt from peering through the darkness. Perhaps Hecate couldn't be trusted, but it was worth trusting for a moment if he could find Ly.

Ly, Ly, Ly, her name pounded in his brain with every footfall. Ly was at the top of the staircase. Ly was going to be saved. Both of them would escape, and he would destroy the gwyllion. She would be safe. His mother would be avenged. The fairytale would end happily ever after. So still he climbed.

Around four hundred steps up, the top of the platform arrived. Numbness tingled in his stiff legs. He collapsed at the top of the stairs and gasped the cool stagnant air for oxygen. His palms pressed against the icy stones.

You're willing to give up now? You're too far in to expect me to keep my promise.

"You're going to hurt me." The words came automatically. He knew she wouldn't hesitate to injure him. He stood, clutching the dagger hidden under his shirt.

Of course I am. You have two minutes until I begin.

He released the dagger's hilt and cracked his knuckles. Then he spun around, throwing himself against the door. It held. He rammed it again with his shoulder. Again, it refused to move. Then he noticed the door handle. He twisted it, and the door swung open to reveal a massive, circular room. A single chandelier hung in the center of the room—which looked like a royal office inside a turret. A massive window through which moonlit snow shown several stories below. When had he gotten above ground? In front of the window sat a plain-looking desk. A staircase ran around the edge of the room, up to a trapdoor in the ceiling.

And on top of the office's desk, lay a girl with blonde hair splayed around her and her hands clasped on top of her unmoving chest.

7

Hecate

Hecate grinned. She couldn't help it—all of this was so amusing. She ought to have guests over more often. They were so much fun. Perhaps after she'd finished with Ly and killed Jackson, she'd have her sister over. It had been a terribly long time since she had seen her.

She did miss her sister. The house spread for miles underneath the forest, burrowing into the earth's crust. It was the way that they were forced to live, in the dark, with massive cities crafted from dirt. Her sister, brother-in-law, and a swarm of nieces and nephews lived so deep under the surface that the youngest of them had never seen sunlight. She was one of the few who lived near the surface without betraying the gwyllion and disappearing into the forest.

If they had the key, though—Jackson's key—everything would change. Unlocking the necklace freed the gwyllion. Families would reunite. The golden reign of the gwyllion would begin.

She fingered the Moonlock. It was a lovely piece, with its careful divots and swirling silver. It was too bad she'd have to destroy it once she unlocked it. Having one's soul bound to a trinket for all of eternity would be rather inconvenient. She studied the body at her feet—her body. At least her original one. She studied the now-closed eyes and frozen face. Yes, she'd been rather pretty. The new form was pretty too, in a different way. Blonde ringlets bounced lightly against her cheeks, and the skin was still pale, but freckles danced across the hands, arms, and face.

The oddest part about taking over the girl's consciousness had to be the height. Perhaps it was a little strange to have sun-kissed skin and blonde hair, but she wasn't standing in front of a mirror. It was most disconcerting to view the walls she had lived in for so long at a different angle. At least the girl's body seemed to be taking well to the magic being woven into her DNA. Had it not, Hecate might have been forced to abandon magic and carry out the final step of her plan with mortal blades.

She smirked to herself. Jackson would likely find her former body. Would he be shocked that she hadn't recovered? Perhaps she should play with him more. Or maybe not let him find it. Being underestimated was good, being presumed dead, however, wasn't Hecate's preferred method of destroying her enemies. She touched the wall and closed her eyes, listening to the musical rhythms of the house. Jackson was still running, searching through the passageway for Ly. What a shock he would have when he found her.

Digging the heel of her palm into the stone, she commanded the house to take her to the office. Light flashed on the other side of the door. Leaving the body and the musty dungeon behind, she entered the new room. Rows of bookshelves lined half of the office's walls, covered lightly in dust. A chandelier swayed from the ceiling. Hecate-Ly climbed onto the desk.

She closed her eyes, pushing Ly's consciousness deeper into the tiny cage in their mind. Then she herself sank into a sleep-like stupor, dragging the house's magic into her, searching the endless, ever-moving passages for her cousin. She pulled magic from where it was the most condensed—and since she and Jackson were the only magic beings this near to the surface, it had to be congregating around him. He was sprinting, and the emotional aspects of magic overwhelmed her with the feelings of his panic.

She smirked. Jackson amused her. It was too bad he would have to die.

The way fae blood combined with human blood amused her. She'd noticed that with the other humans that occasionally came around. Even those with a single drop of fae blood felt everything so strongly, at least a dozen times more deeply than pure humans felt. They also fell in love fast and hard. They couldn't help themselves.

And that inability to prevent it made Jackson's search a hundred times funnier.

She whispered to him, manipulating him with her words as she did to the house with her mind. She felt his emotions from a distance. Then she commanded the house itself.

She listened for a moment as the house replied to Jackson's panicked words, taunting him, whispering regrets and fury. This was the most fun she'd had in quite a while. Guests were so pleasing to have over, mortals especially so. It was quite disappointing that she had other appointments. She'd see Jackson soon, though, so she barely had to wait for the continuation of her amusement.

Her eyelids fluttered as she pulled herself from the endless sleep. It would take time for Jackson to climb the stairs to the room, time she did not want to waste. She pushed herself to a sitting position and spun to the side, dangling her legs and leaning back on her arms. It had been far too long since one of her plans had culminated so smoothly. She almost felt bad for Jackson and his naivete, the ease with which he'd fallen into her trap.

She kicked one leg out and swung it back. Ly's pants were rather comfortable. Perhaps she ought to get some when this was all over. She yawned.

Jackson, it seemed, was slower than she had expected. It must be his human blood interfering. If only he would use magic, but he refused. The light fae had convinced him that magic wielded by a child of a gwyllion must be dark. Hecate rolled her eyes. She was sure that the light fae refused to talk about how their queen two generations ago had been a former gwyllion. Foolish fae.

Time ticked by, minutes upon minutes. Surely Jackson was climbing the stairs. She knew the house had made it obvious for him. Was he possibly that dense to have not noticed it?

Panting rose up the stairs. Hecate-Ly resumed her position on the table, hair splayed around a still face. She touched the dagger hidden in the waist of her pants. Pants truly surpassed skirts in every way. When her people were freed, the women ought to be allowed to wear pants.

She slipped the necklace under the collar of Ly's sweater. The plan was going swimmingly. She smiled to herself, then folded her arms over her chest and let her consciousness drift out of her body and throughout the castle, tethered only by the restraints of the Moonlock. Only when Hecate-Ly's body woke up would she be forced to return to the mortal constraints.

She commanded a staircase to spiral around the inside of the tower. Bookshelves disappeared as the staircase led up to a trapdoor appearing in the ceiling. Two chairs formed beside a low coffee table. The room smelled like cinnamon. Hecate commanded the house to freeze. She trembled with excitement. Within the hour, her people would be freed. They could return to the towns they once roamed in, feasting on the blood of the humans. They could thrive.

Something thudded at the top of the stairs. She rolled her eyes. *Finally.* Except nothing came after the thud. Really? Jackson managed to arrive, even after he'd endured her traps, just to give up? He really was more emotional than she had initially suspected.

"You're really willing to give up now?" She took control of the house's voice—her voice—with a smile. "You're in too far to expect me to keep my promise."

"You're going to hurt me." His words were faint from the other side of the door, but loud enough for her to hear.

"Of course I am." The smirk penetrated her words. "You have two minutes until I begin."

There was a moment of silence, then something slammed into the door, causing the wood to creak under the weight. Then another bang, before the handle turned and the door swung open. Jackson stood on the threshold of the room, sweat pouring from his forehead and glasses askew. If he had been paying attention, he might have seen the ghostly form of his cousin perched on the stairs.

But he wasn't.

His gaze focused on Ly's body. Three strides later, he stood over her frozen form. His fingers caressed her cold cheek, then he leaned down and pressed his lips against hers.

Pain shot through Hecate as she was sucked back into Ly's body. She gasped, then blinked, staring up into her cousin's too-close face. Then she smiled.

Jackson really was more emotional than she thought.

8

Jackson

He had kissed her. He hadn't meant to. It had kind of just happened. Maybe it was the magic in him that said the only way to wake the fair maiden was with a kiss, or maybe it was just the fact that she looked so pretty lying there and was possibly dead and he panicked because he had never actually seen a dead *human* before. The pureblood fae crumbled into ash within minutes of their deaths. Dead bodies weren't a common sight, and someone lying so still and cold was terrifying.

Either way, he had kissed her. His lips tingled with the sensation and his heart pounded in his ears. He shouldn't have done that. He was a respectable gentleman, not someone who assaulted a sleeping lady with kisses. *Hades*, he had really done that, hadn't he?

Her eyelids fluttered open.

His voice caught in his throat. His face flushed. "I—I didn't mean to, Ly. I'm so sorry. I should have asked."

She smiled.

He shook his head. "That was terrible of me. I should never have forced myself onto you. That was incredibly rude and unchivalrous."

"It's okay." She grinned. It was a cute, lopsided grin that made the freckles on her nose scrunch. "I've always wanted to be kissed."

Jackson licked his lips and tried to recompose himself. The kiss was still warm on his breath. The corners of his mouth tugged into a smile. This was embarrassing. "I should have asked."

"No, you oughtn't have." Ly shrugged. "It's really okay."

The grief and panic clouding everything moments before hit like a tidal wave. She was okay. She was alive and in front of him and not rotting away in some box deep inside the castle. Tears burned the corners of his eyes. "Are you okay?" He hesitated. How weird would it be to tell her he thought she'd died in a little box? "You're not hurt?"

"No." She shook her head, curls bouncing. "I got a little turned around and found a secret passage, but everything is okay. This house is really neat."

"You didn't get squished in any... boxes?"

Her eyebrows knit. Jackson stared at her. Her eyes were really, really blue. He liked blue eyes. "Boxes?"

"Like..." He gestured a cube with his hands. "Box."

She laughed. Full-on laughed at him. Her cheeks turned rosy. His did, too, but for a completely different reason. She grinned at him. "No, no boxes."

"Oh, okay." He pushed his glasses up on his nose. "Good. I'm glad there weren't any boxes."

She snorted. "Yup. I'm hungry."

"Yeah." Jackson ran a hand through his hair. Why did he have to feel so awkward? "Me too."

"The food upstairs wasn't filling." She slid off the desk, landing with a bounce. "Who serves guests only brownies when it's at least dinner time?"

Jackson hadn't noticed how short she was before. She was pretty, button nose, round cheeks, and petite frame. Very pixie-like. He wondered if maybe she had a bit of fairy blood too. "Whoever owns this house, I guess. And it was, like, two A.M."

"Who owns it?" She ran her fingers through her curls, as if she were trying to straighten them. "It's just been here forever if I remember right."

He smirked. "You remember forever?"

"I remember five hours ago when we didn't eat enough and so now our stomachs are growling."

Had it only been five hours? Jackson shook his head. How had he managed to go from being slightly annoyed at her to kissing her in five hours? Sure, she was the first human girl to pay much attention to him, but he had interacted with girls before. He wasn't a tease, and he didn't flirt and develop crushes on girls in a matter of hours. What was wrong with him? Was it the lack of sleep? Or that his mother died?

The thought slammed into his gut. He'd forgotten. He'd forgotten that his mother died and then the reminder swept him off of his feet until he was tumbling back down the staircase into the pit of despair. He'd been so swept up in Ly being alive that his mother dying had completely disappeared from his mind.

But the memory returned in a rush. Tears welled in his eyes.

Ly's eyes widened. "What's wrong? Did I do something wrong?'

He shook his head. "No, no. I'm sorry. I found out that my mother died a little while ago. It just... kind of... It hits over and over again."

"Oh, oh my goodness. That's awful. I can't believe it. That's horrible, I'm so sorry." She reached up and rubbed his shoulder. "How did it happen?"

"My cousin." Jackson took a deep, shuddering breath, suppressing the furious tears and the scream begging to be released. He wanted Hecate to pay. He wanted to make her regret every action she'd ever made. But that would be the behavior of a gwyllion. He hated this flurry of feelings. "My cousin killed my mother."

Ly's jaw dropped. "Oh. My. Gosh. I'm so sorry. Is he going to go to jail? For killing your mom?"

"She... no. It doesn't work that way." He needed to explain the fae so she could protect herself. He needed to reveal why he really visited the old house. He reached for her hand. She let him take it. Then, gently, as if she was a fawn ready to bolt, Jackson led her over to the two chairs in the corner. "Okay, I need to explain something. It's going to sound crazy. I'm going to sound crazy. I'm not crazy, I promise. At least, I'm probably not."

She hadn't stopped smiling since he grabbed her hand. "I love crazy."

"Uh... okay. So you know, like, the fae in Scottish myths?"

She bobbed her head. "Yeah, what about them?"

"Well, there are these bad fae called gwyllion—they're kind of like vampires, but with more magic abilities." He suddenly felt shaky. Why was he telling her this? She was going to hate him. She would think he was crazy—after he'd kissed her, too. "Uh, so my biological mother was one of them, and she died, so the queen of the light fae—Elvira—adopted me. So, yeah. I'm part fae, and I was raised by them. And—"

"We aren't in Scotland though." Ly's pale eyebrows knitted, confusion spreading across her features. "How in the world are Scottish fae over here?'

"They immigrated during the 1600s, along with pure humans. They intermarried a lot with the humans at first. About half of normal humans are also a little bit fae." *Hades,* he was rambling again. "Pureblood fae—especially the dark ones—were confined to the forests centuries ago so that only the bravest humans would have to face them. The magic necklace that kept them in the forest would kill every dark fae if destroyed. But with the right key, the locket would be unlocked and they would go free. I'm here to destroy the Moonlock and the key so that humans won't be in danger anymore from the gwyllion."

"Oh. Hm." She nodded slowly. "Why can't the dark fae be released?"

He paused. ". . .because they're like vampires. They'd suck the blood out of every human and hybrid in the world until there was nothing left but bloodless corpses. Y'know how there aren't any animals in the woods? It's because of the gwyllion. They ate them all."

Ly cringed. "Graphic, much?"

"Sorry." He coughed. "Basically they'd lay ruin to the world."

"Oh."

"Yeah."

Awkward silence lay thick in the room for a few long minutes. Ly took the information far better than Jackson had expected her to. He'd been bracing for some kind of shock or fear or disbelief. She seemed more worried about a PG-13 description of violence. He studied her face. She stared at her hands, her chest rising and falling with slow breaths. So few humans knew about the fae, yet she acted so casual about it. It was a little strange.

"Can I see the key?"

He blinked. "Huh?"

"The key. You're trying to destroy the bad fae, right?"

"Oh." He nodded. "Yeah, I'm destroying that at the same time. Make everything more final."

"I know. You told me. Can I see it?"

Jackson glanced around the room. Hecate was in the house, somewhere. She might have followed him—but he hadn't heard her voice since he entered the room. *Hades*, he had forgotten about her two-minute warning. Surely it had been two minutes. "Yeah, really quick. We need to get out of here before my cousin returns."

Ly watched him with interest as he pulled a dagger out of its sheath at his side. The intricate design of the blade glistened in the chandelier's light. Jackson laid his hand over the blade and pulled it back with a key in his palm. The indent of the key's former hiding spot cast shadows over the design. Jackson laid it on his other knee and resheathed the dagger. "Here it is."

"Why did you kiss me?" Ly stared into his eyes, a fierceness present that had not been apparent earlier.

He had to admit, he was not expecting that question. The heat of a blush crawled up his neck. "I saw you lying there dead, and in the stories... true love's kiss... you know."

She snorted. "You're tongue-tied."

He schooled his features. "It was an unexpected question."

"Not as unexpected as you kissing me."

"Yeah." He took off his glasses and rubbed them on the hem of his shirt. He glanced up at Ly. Wow, was his vision improving? She looked really clear. Wait, his shirt was still wet. He groaned and looked at the lenses. Smear-marks covered the glasses, and he slipped them on. Sure enough, his vision was obscured. "Sorry about that."

She touched his knee with a smile. "I'm teasing you, Jackson."

"What?" He frowned. "What did you say?"

Her smile faltered, and her gaze fell to her lap. "I'm teasing you. I'm sorry. I wasn't trying to hurt your feelings."

"No, no." Jackson shook his head, his hand creeping towards the key on his leg. "After that."

"I said Jackson. I said your name."

"That's the problem." Jackson wasn't sure whether to grab the key or his dagger. "Why did you decide to start calling me by my name... now?"

"Oh."

"Yeah." He decided on the dagger.

Ly dove for the key. He reached to stop her, but it was already firmly clasped in her hands as she knelt beside him. He raised his dagger. She froze, her large eyes widening. He hesitated, but that hesitation was all she needed to smile and leap to her feet, then sprint up the stairs surrounding the office.

9

Hecate

Hecate gasped for breath, struggling to force air into her lungs. Fae could survive on just a little oxygen. A mortal body in the process of transforming into fae still needed air. Her thighs burned as she scaled step after step. With the sharp drop to her right, the railingless stairs became more and more dangerous. Fairies didn't die naturally, but gravity didn't count as natural. And if Ly's body were to fall, would Hecate die along with it? She ought to have read the fine print for the necklace and her powers.

But she hadn't, so she just clung to the wall, hoping that she didn't slip and drop to her and Ly's deaths. Jackson matched her pace, just a few feet behind her, but she turned around and smirked. She had the high ground, and she stared him down. He stopped, brandishing his dagger.

"You really shouldn't run with sharp objects. You might get hurt."

He waved his dagger. "Who are you?"

"I'm Ly, of course."

"Get out of Ly's head." His voice cracked. "Get out of her head right now."

Hecate-Ly chuckled and backed up a step. "I think you will have to elaborate."

Frustration wrinkled Jackson's forehead. "I don't know if you're mind controlling or possessing or shapeshifting to look like her. I don't even know who you are. But you look like the girl I'm in love with and the girl I'm in love with would never steal a key and try to kill me."

"Then you hardly know the girl you are 'in love' with."

Jackson gestured with the dagger. "I know you aren't her."

"Congratulations, you are observant." Hecate-Ly pushed a curl out of her face.

Jackson pushed up his glasses and rubbed his eye with his free hand. His eyes were red and sleepy and matched the aesthetic of his bony form. "Who are you and why are you trying to kill me?"

"*You're* the one chasing me."

"Just give me back the key, Ly. Please."

"Now why would I want to do that, cousin."

Jackson's jaw dropped and his eyebrow rose before he schooled his features back into pure rage. His knuckles whitened on his blade. His jaw clenched. She smirked and tilted her head, but she positioned herself to turn and run.

"Hecate." He spat the name.

"I guess you've won our little guessing game."

"Get out of Ly's head." There was an undertone of pleading. "Let that be the prize."

"No, you just get boasting rights." She winked.

Anger morphed back to shock and then disgust. "I kissed you."

"Technically, you kissed Ly." She struggled to suppress her laughter. The entire situation amused her. "But yes."

"Please, Hecate. Get out of her head."

She felt the silver smoke of her magic swirling between each finger. More of Ly's body was becoming fae with every passing second. "Why would I do that? Even in a mortal body, I have everything I need." She smirked and used her keyless hand to pull the necklace from under Ly's sweater collar. "Everything I need to free our people."

"Your people."

"You cannot deny your bloodline, cousin."

"Dark fae changed their bloodline into gwyllion. I can change mine back."

She chuckled and fingered the Moonlock. Perhaps he was right. It wouldn't matter in the end. She could unlock the necklace here and now, inside the house that had so terribly imprisoned them. But there would be a sort of poetic justice to wait to be out in the forest, to see the magic barriers vanish and freedom become reality. "Perhaps, cousin. You would still destroy your people. And now that your girlfriend—"

"She's not my girlfriend."

"You kissed her, Jackson."

Jackson's face scrunched. "I didn't know she was you—you were her. You were in her head and needed to get the Hades out of there."

"I could have stopped you," Hecate tilted the necklace in the light and watched it sparkle. Jackson still hadn't acknowledged it. She longed for his shock and horror. She lifted her key and traced the edge of the locket. "I even ought to've, but it all happened so fast, cousin."

"Stop." The shock didn't exist on his pale features. More anger, years of it, cracked the surface of his stoic façade. Tears threatened to spill and stain his still-damp shirt. He pointed the blade at her heart.

Hecate suppressed a snort. Jackson could never hurt his 'true love,' even if someone else was occupying the girl's body. She noticed it in the way he licked his lips, in the tremble of his hand holding the dagger. Jackson genuinely loved Ly and would save her if there was the slightest chance of surviving. Thus, Hecate knew that the body she currently possessed would be unharmed by her cousin.

"Now, Hecate." His voice shifted from pleading to commanding. "Get out of her head now."

"Eheheh," she smiled at him. "That'd be a wonderful idea. Really a brilliant concept for you to suggest, Jackson. Too bad brilliance runs in the family."

"What?"

"Once I figured out Ly was on a scavenger hunt, it only took a few readjustments of the game to lead her straight to me."

Jackson cringed. He should have known. He did know, yet he did nothing to stop it. The stairs creaked as he took yet another step forward. She backed up two stairs, avoiding the sight of the steep drop beside her. If she could get to the trapdoor at the end of the staircase, she'd be outside. She'd open the locket. Her people would be freed.

Blue electricity crackled around Jackson's fingertips and crawled up his blade. "Do it. You heard me the first time."

"Losing control of your powers now, are you?" She knitted her eyebrows, assumed a taunting expression to hide the fear flaming in her chest. Rogue magic endangered everyone nearby, and the first lesson the gwyllion learned was to control—control their emotions, control their situation, control their magic. Control everything they could because the light fae had taken everything. But if Jackson refused to assume control of his magic, it could ruin everything.

"Give me the key and get out of her head."

Hecate tilted her head. "I think not. Perhaps the light fae do not teach how trading works. It is an *exchange*. One thing for another. You have nothing to give me, yet expect me to give you two?"

"I won't kill you right here if you do it." More blue sparks. She grimaced. She needed to calm him. If she could instill fear, his power would subside. Anger only blew things up—quite literally.

"Perhaps." She commanded her smoke to increase and billow around her, pouring down the stairs, ensnaring his feet, cascading off the thirty-foot drop beside her. "But as soon as you have the key, you will kill me and confiscate the necklace. You don't need the key, anyways."

The sparks grew, engulfing Jackson's hands in blue light. This was dangerous. The smoke dissolved. If Jackson lost control, both of them would land on stone floors with shattered bones, at best. Dead, at worst. She spun and sprinted up the stairs. Jackson's steps fell heavy behind her, just slightly slower than her rhythm, but nearly keeping pace with her. She locked her sights on the platform two-dozen steps away, willing it to come closer. But the house heeded a previous command and remained still, the unmoving platform out of her reach. She climbed, slowing with each step until Jackson was right on her heels. Fingers closed around her wrist, but she jerked away. With a grunt, she darted up the ladder leading to the flat roof of the house's tower and shoved open the trap door. *Outside.* She hadn't been out of the house's labyrinth in a decade.

A hand gripped her ankle. She squirmed, but Jackson refused to release her. His clasp tightened as she grasped at the snow. She flung her leg back. It collided with something hard; there was a crunch and a grunt of pain. Jackson's grip faltered enough for her to escape. She shoved the trap-door all the way open and climbed out onto the flat roof. The icy wind sent snowflakes across her skin, not melting on fae-possessed flesh. She stepped lightly across the snow, leaving no prints as she moved across the roof to behind the trap door.

She pulled the dagger from its hidden sheath and slipped the key into her pocket. She would take care of it in a moment. Right now she needed to focus on her cousin. He would be dead before he made it onto the roof. Jackson's head popped out from the trap door. Hecate lunged as Jackson leaped from the trap door, barely dodging her knife.

Scarlet blood gushed from his nose, staining the snow an intense red. He backed up against the small ledge—the only thing between him and an eighty-foot plummet into the snowy ground. Hecate grinned. This would be too easy. She glanced over her shoulder, checking to make sure that she had a landing ten feet below on the snow-padded angle of the lower rooftop.

She hadn't expected a body to be flung at her, nearly knocking her onto that landing pad. She twisted around, to see Jackson on top of her. His nose was askew, still pouring blood across his face and now soiling her shirt.

His words came in thick, whispered breaths as steam poured from his lips. "Get out of her head."

"No." Hecate blew a steamy breath into his face.

Pain shattered through her body, jolting her muscles. Stars zoomed across her vision and she bit back a scream. Her hands seized up, and the sound of buzzing grew louder and louder until it felt like her ears were going to explode. Her arms ached and her entire body vibrated with the electric shocks. She kept her gaze locked on Jackson's furious face. His eyes flickered blue every time he sent a new surge of electricity through her. Unbridled fury rarely ended smoothly. He was going to kill her

"It's Ly's body." The words barely dropped from her lips when a new flash of blinding shock fizzled through her. But it was cut short. Hecate blinked back the sharp tingles still stabbing her body.

"What did you say?" Jackson wiped blood from his face, grimacing under the pain.

"It's Ly's body," Hecate whispered. The ringing still echoed in her ears. "If you destroy it, she'll be gone forever."

Jackson pushed himself to his feet. Chill bumps speckled his arms, and his clothes were dark from melting snow. The half-human part of him made the rest of him soaked and cold. He scrutinized Hecate-Ly. "I can't kill you."

"If you destroy me," Hecate's muscles still ached, but she forced herself to stand as well. Something was satisfying about the expression on his face—one of despair and frustration. "You destroy her, too."

"Give me back the key."

"No." Hecate flexed her hand as her powers healed Ly's body from the electric shocks. "I don't think I will."

She pushed herself to her feet, bracing her body against the wall. She grabbed her necklace in one hand and pulled the key from where she'd slipped it in Ly's pocket. Freedom was seconds away. Her people would live again. She inserted the key into the center of the Moonlock.

The spell billowed on her lips, the charm to open the necklace and free her people. She whispered the words, dark smoke billowing from her fingers as she turned the key. A smile spread across her lips. This was it, they would be free. The last phrase was on the edge of her lips when—

Something slammed into her stomach. Gasping, she reached for the wall but overestimated its height. Everything spun as she fell. Pain shattered through her before everything went dark.

10

Jackson

Ly's blonde hair formed a halo around her still form. Bile mixed with blood in the back of Jackson's throat. Was Hecate dead? Was Ly? He'd already failed to save her from his cousin. Now he had killed her—the little of her that might be left after Hecate's attack.

He needed her to live again. He needed to get down and save her and revive her. Or maybe she wasn't dead. If he could break the locket, Hecate would die, but Ly might still be trapped inside of her head, the shrinking box crushing her. His nose throbbed as the blood poured down his face. Why hadn't he been more careful? She wouldn't be in this situation if he hadn't helped her find the secret staircase behind the fireplace in the first place.

He dashed to the other side of the tower; it was almost a ten-foot drop to the steeply slanted roof, but there was no other way for him to quickly access her body. He couldn't navigate the entire house again in search of an exit. So he jumped.

The jolt of his landing pained his nose more than any other part of his body. The snow cushioned his fall and he dug his heels into the white powder to keep from slipping. The ground was another sixty or so feet from the edge of the angled roof, so jumping wasn't an option. He needed to be by her side. He felt the seconds ticking by—the seconds he could use to save the little bit of Ly being crushed in her head.

So he scrambled to the edge of the roof. His foot slipped as he dropped and landed face-first onto a snow-padded balcony. Whether she'd done it intentionally or not, Hecate had allowed the house to make a perfect stairway for him to reach Ly. Sharp pain jolted through his nose, leaving streaks of blood in the snow, but he climbed over the edge of the balcony and sprung to a lower one.

Hecate. The name stung inside his head, swirling with red disbelief. How could she do such a thing? Killing someone, feasting on blood was one evil, stealing someone's body and manipulating it while her soul was being crushed inside her head was a completely different level. Anger boiled in his blood as his feet crunched against the crystals on the ground. She had possessed Ly, let him kiss her, and then stolen the key from him. It was brilliant, really, but in the most awful way he could imagine. And he wanted to scream.

Electricity tingled in his palms, reminding him to take a deep breath of the cool winter air. Snowflakes drifted lightly as he rounded the side corner of the house. The snow slowed his steps, but the thick flakes only reached the middle of his calf. Ly could easily have made it home in these conditions. Why had he had to insist that they would be forced to stay two days? He could have saved her right at the beginning. Alas, the future stayed invisible to the fae. He couldn't have known—but if he had. . . Maybe he could have driven her out of there, he could have made sure she made it home safe and sound. What he wouldn't give to walk her home right now. . .

Then he was beside her. There was no movement to her body. Already her skin started turning to match her lifeless eyes. No breaths misted off her cold lips. True love's kiss wouldn't save her this time.

Jackson stared at the body as snowflakes melted on the not-yet-frozen skin. A tear tickled his cheek. Why? Why did Ly have to be the one who made it to the end of this scavenger hunt first? Why couldn't he have fought Hecate when he had the chance—he should have known she'd have the locket on her.

He knelt down in the snow to pick up the chain lying beside her—the necklace had become unlatched in the fall, and the key had broken free, landing a few feet away in the snow. Jackson snatched it from where it laid. With a grunt, he shoved the wrong end of the key into the keyhole of the moon, preparing to use the leverage to destroy the piece of jewelry.

And then he felt a barely substantial hand on his wrist.

A ghostly form of Hecate stood before him, dark smoke creating her figure. Her voice was breathy, nearly lost in the winter's breeze. Dark circles stained the smoke under her eyes. She had the look of a corpse. She almost looked more dead than Ly's body on the ground. "Please, Jackson. Don't do it. Don't destroy us."

He didn't want the sympathy that sparked in his heart. "You killed an innocent person, Hecate. My person. Hades knows that the first person you kill is the hardest."

Tears formed in her misty eyes. "My people will die. Kill me if you choose, but we're not all like that."

"Hecate, I lived with the gwyllion until I was eight. I know, for a fact, that all of you are like that."

Hecate's teary façade faded. "Do not do it. Ly will die."

Jackson shoved the end of the key like a lever.

It shocked him how easily the locket snapped in two. The face of the moon popped right off, falling into the snow lightly. Smoke poured from the broken halves, darker than Hecate's, that warming his skin. He watched it for a moment, as it changed from obsidian to grey, before lightening to a pure, snowy white and dispersing in the freezing air.

He raised his gaze to where Hecate's ghost had been moments before. A faint shimmer hung in the air where her form had stood, but she was gone. Dead. He supposed he should feel some kind of shame. He had almost expected to die with them, as he was one of the gwyllion. But maybe in the same way a good fae could become dark, he had become good. Maybe he had only survived because of Elvira. There was no maybe about it. He would be dead without his mother.

His eyes lingered on Ly's dead form. Should he bury her body? He realized with a touch of shock that he didn't know if she had a family. What should he do—waltz into town declaring he'd found a girl's body in the woods when she'd barely been missing 24 hours? The blame would immediately fall on him. When they tested her body, he wasn't even sure they'd find that she was human. Who knew what Hecate had done to Ly's DNA?

He knelt beside the body in the snow. He placed a hand over her heart. It didn't beat. He knew it wouldn't, but he had hoped—his chest tightened as a tingling crawled up his hand. There was a flash of hope in his mind. He could save her. Breaths could fly off her beautiful lips again. He would see her smile.

But it would come at a cost. Leaning back, he sat on the balls of his feet. She, as a human, was dead. But she could be a fae. It was difficult to do, even with full fae magic. Jackson wasn't sure if he could pull it off. He inspected her twisted figure briefly before placing one hand on her neck and the other on her stomach. Sparks crackled around his fingers. He took a deep breath and closed his eyes

Breathe, Ly. Breathe. Beat, heart. Embrace the fae. Become a fae.

He opened his eyes. *Nothing.* Disappointment and frustration swirled in him. This wasn't fair to her. She shouldn't be dead. He wanted her alive. He needed her alive. So he tried again.

I think I love you, Ly. Please wake up. He paused his internal speech to look at her body. Nothing. *Ly, wake up. Right now. This is... Jumping-jack speaking. Please wake up.*

Two tears slid down his cheeks, melting as they hit the snow. *Wake up, Ly. Wake up, please.*

And then he kissed her. Again. It was a desperate kiss as his lips touched hers. He did love her... or he was beginning to. He wanted to love her. At the very least, he wanted her to not be dead. *Please, Ly. Please become a fae. Please wake up.*

He didn't realize he was cradling her body until he opened his eyes. Her golden hair spilled down across his arms, seeming to glow in the now-setting sun. Except it wasn't seeming to glow. It was glowing. Her entire body glowed faintly with a fae-light. He let go of her, shock shaking his limbs. Her body slipped to the snow at the same moment a lightly steamed breath blew off her lips. For the briefest of seconds, he was thankful for Hecate's morphing of her DNA. Ly lived. She was a fae, but she lived.

Jackson jumped to his feet, and though he wouldn't admit it later, he most certainly yelled in delight.

11

Ly

This wasn't a box. She wasn't being crushed. There was something besides smothering darkness. Everything besides smothering darkness. There was light, the setting sun bouncing off of the snow. Wind whistling through the glade. Trees lined the edges of her peripheral vision, both the spindly skeletons of the summer trees and the thick emerald of the evergreen.

And breathing! The icy air whooshed into her lungs. She wasn't suffocating. She breathed. Even lying against the snow, paralyzed, her limbs were warm. A power and a lightness pulsed through her veins in a way she'd never felt before.

Her eyes focused on the teenage boy whooping and jumping in the snow beside her. What was Jimmy doing leaping around?

Movement returned to her limbs, sending a tingling wave through her muscles. She pushed herself up and sat watching him as he kicked the flakes and watched them drift back to the ground. He spun around and fell backward into the calf-high snow with a *shpumph*. Ly grinned and stood with the intent of drudging through the snow to him, but the snow stayed underneath her instead of becoming quicksand. Weird, why wasn't she sinking? Maybe it was just thinner over here.

She walked over to Joe and peered down at him.

He grinned back up at her. "You're alive."

"You betcha." She offered him a hand, which he took, and pulled him to his feet.

He hugged her.

Heat burned in her cheeks. Her pulse fluttered but she continued standing awkwardly, grinning like a complete idiot. "What's this for?"

He let go and walked over to one of the snowdrifts, which he perched lightly on with legs crossed. "Just happy you're alive."

She sat down beside him and tilted her head. "I think you're not from around here."

Something changed just slightly in his expression before returning to the joy and relief from before. "Why's that?"

"Well," she leaned back, her bare palms resting against the snow. Shouldn't her hands be numb by now? "It wasn't snowing that hard earlier. Like, it was snowing a lot— but I could have made it home. I thought you might have seen a forecast or something, and I've always been too trusting—" *Why did he just snort?* "You must be from the South or something."

"South Carolina, actually." He shrugged. "Weather can be dramatic. I didn't know."

"It can." She bobbed her head. "What happened while I was being crushed?"

He raised an eyebrow. "Crushed?"

"Inside my head. In the box."

"Oh." His eyes seem to stare into her soul. "What do you last remember?"

"The necklace." Ly shivered, but not from the cold. The suffocating feeling swept over her, the feeling that she was not in control as the darkness filled her lungs and her head until she was very, very small. "I put on the necklace because she told me to. And then she was in my head and locked me in there. In the box that tried to crush me."

"Yeah." Jackson traced a figure eight into the snow with his left pointer finger. "Yeah, that girl was my cousin."

"Your *cousin?*" Ly's eyes widened. "Your cousin tried to kill me?"

"She did kill you, Ly."

Ly's eyes widened even more. She looked down at her hands. A faint sheen of sparkles glinted in the last sun rays. "Am I a ghost?!"

Jackson ran a hand through his dark hair. "Uh, no. You're a fae."

"So I'm not dead? I thought you said she killed me."

"You're a freaking fae, Ly. You're alive."

Ly tugged on a curl. "Are you sure? Am I not a little bit dead?"

"You don't care that you're now a magical, traditionally supernatural being?"

"Ohh," Ly nodded. "That's how you kept me alive."

"Yes," He mirrored her, nodding. "Yeah, it is."

She kicked at the snow with her feet. *A fae*, she'd heard the word before, but she couldn't remember exactly what it meant.

Maybe her mom had read her a bedtime story about them before. And supernatural? Like, magical? She stared at the snow and the stark contrast of the black mansion. How could she be a fae? Maybe he was joking. "What's a fae?"

Why did Jackson look so uncomfortable? He frowned. "Well, I'm part fae. It's like... sometimes people call them fairies. And they're magical."

"But I'm not a fairy."

"You weren't." Jackson's focus drifted back to the pattern in the snow. He traced it again and again and again. It was relaxing to watch. "I had to make you one."

"A fairy?"

"Yeah."

"You're one?"

"Yeah." He rubbed his nose, which was slightly red from the cold. He had a very nice-shaped nose, just the right amount of pointed, but not so sharp he looked mean.

"What's it like to be a fairy?"

"It's a lot of..." He hesitated, trying to think of the right word. "Fighting evil. I was— am— the fairy queen's adopted son. She trained me to protect humans and fae."

"Oh." Ly nodded like she understood. She somewhat did this time. It all sounded familiar. "Did you tell me this before?"

"I explained it to Hecate when she was in your body."

"I think I might have heard it then." She twisted a curl around her fingers. "Is that why you saved me? So I didn't die?"

"Not exactly." Now Jackson's whole face flushed scarlet. "I wanted you alive."

"Why?"

He took a deep breath. "Because I think I love you. I didn't mean to. Fae fall in love fast."

"Oh." She stared into the snow. That, of all things, was not what she expected him to say. She liked him too, a little bit. Something in her stomach churned. Just a little bit. "Do I get magic?"

Glass shattered behind her. She turned, staring up at the massive house. She could have sworn it had grown. A hand closed around her wrist. Movement to her right caught her eye, as Jackson leaped to his feet, tugging her up with him. But she stood still, transfixed. Glass rained from the top windows, puncturing the snow like bullets. Then the next floor's windows shattered and dropped, and then the following floor's. Soon all the windows were empty. The wind picked up, whistling through the bare house.

And the siding fell. It crashed to the ground, black splinters and grey stones mingling with the glass. The shingles came flying down. In the span of a minute, the house turned into a skeleton. His grip was tight on her wrist, and she held his tightly.

"Ly," Jackson's voice shook. "Run."

They sprinted into the forest. Crashes echoed behind them and the snow slipped backward so that they seemed to be on a treadmill, barely escaping the black hole of the house. Trees rushed past them, sinking into the abyss. The snow dragged at their feet, trying to pull them with it. Ly's right leg ached like she had run a marathon. She was just slightly faster than

Jackson, pulling him along. Her knuckles were white on his wrist.

His hand slipped. "Let me go; we'll be faster separated."

"Really?" She barely had enough breath to pant the word. Something told her not to obey him, but that thought fled quickly.

"Yeah."

So she let go. He fell behind. She spun around. The snow dragged at her feet, but she remained standing. Jackson, on the other hand, was face first, slipping into the deep cavern created by the collapsing house. Something surged through her bones, stronger than adrenaline, stronger, even, than the power of the collapsing house.

Her muscles pulsed. The pain in her leg disappeared as she dodged the sliding trees and rocks and ran towards Jackson. The fear whispering in her head was dismissed. She needed to get to him. He had saved her life, now it was her turn. Sliding past one last tree trunk, she reached him. He lifted an arm, and she grabbed it, dragging him from the avalanche.

As soon as Jackson stood on the snow, the crumbling stopped. The house was gone, and in its place was a massive, snow-filled crater.

Ly coughed. "What was that?"

"The magic of the house self-destructed," he panted. "Also, excuse me for a moment, I need to throw up."

Ly turned her back on him and studied the desecrated landscape. Most of the trees that she had walked by all her life no longer stood upright. Some of them had completely fallen, sunk into the pit where the house had been. Others simply grew horizontally out of the earth. She tilted her head to look at them.

What had happened there, just a minute ago? She wasn't athletic. Her running was rather impressive, considering that the last time she worked out was when she was four and doing it with her parents. Was that display of strength some of the fae magic that Jackson has said? Part of her wondered if he was just crazy. But what he said *made sense.* Giddy excitement swirled through her. She could be magical. She might be a fairy.

"So…"

She spun around. Jackson had walked up behind her. His face was pale and his eyes bloodshot. Ly gasped. "What happened?"

"Hecate said destroying the Moonlock would make me sick." He frowned at the snow. "I need to sit down."

He rested in the snow, and Ly plopped down beside him. "Shouldn't being a fae keep you from getting sick or something?"

"Not when it's tied to the magic."

"Oh." She looked him over. His limbs were thin, his body frail like a twig in a windstorm. "Y'know, I don't think you can go back to fairyland like that."

"It's called the Glade." He coughed, and then continued coughing for a minute. When he pulled his arm away from his mouth, blood speckled the jacket of his elbow. "Also, you're going to have to come with me, now that you're a fae."

Ly didn't like that idea. At all. If she came with him, her mom would be concerned. A burst of adrenaline pumped through her veins. She'd have to leave her family. Leaving her family was the last thing she wanted to do; she planned to start her art business so she didn't have to go off to college. She'd have to cross that bridge when she came to it, though. "How far away is it?"

"A good little ways away. The mountains of South Carolina."

"Well," Ly boosted herself to her feet. The lack of cold in the snow was a strange sensation. "You're in no position to travel."

Jackson snorted and stood, too. Immediately his feet seemed to slide out from under him, and he stumbled forward. He landed face-first in the snow. Ly jumped forward and helped him up. Blood streamed down his face; his nose had started bleeding again. His expression wasn't fully there, glazed over and tired.

Ly tucked her arm under his. "Yeah, you definitely can't travel right now. Come with me."

He leaned on her for support. "Where are we going?"

"To my house. We'll help get you better there. Then we can travel."

She was surprised at his lack of resistance. Steps in sync, they trudged up the snowdrifts, supporting each other when they slipped until they reached where the snow flattened out and the woods didn't sink into the ground. The full moon shone through the forest bows, glistening like pixie dust on the snow. Side-by-side they made their way out of the forest, warmed by each other, comforted with the village's lights in the distance.

The End

Acknowledgements

It never made sense to me when authors thanked so many people in the acknowledgements in the back of their books until I've published my own. Holding this book, you never would guess how many people are invested in it.

So thank you to Mom and Dad for being patient with me for all the times I said I would get to the dishes in five minutes. And thank you to my sisters, SE, Ali, LB, and LK for being (mostly) quiet when I was writing. (Also, thank you Mother Dearest for helping with the editing. I seriously couldn't have done that part without you.)

Thank you to Kellen, Gracie, Nina, and Lin for reading the first (and second, and third) drafts of this book. It would not be nearly where it is today without the four of you.

Ann and Nathan, thank you for the encouragement you've given me. I probably wouldn't have kept going without the two of you. Thanks to the rest of Infinity, too. This story wouldn't exist without the short-story contest the seven of us put on so many months ago.

Darcy, thank you for spinning worlds with your words while helping around our house when I was little. The stories you told inspired me to tell my own.

And thank you to Jenna Terese, Grace A. Johnson, Lauren D. Fulter, and all the other indie authors that answered my endless questions and helped me learn how to publish independently.

Lastly, thank You, God, for giving me the imagination and opening up so many opportunities to write. Thank you for drawing me to You through this process and teaching me to trust You with my hopes and dreams.

About the Author

To find an E. K. Seaver, you must set a trap. The best option is to lure her in using chocolate, blankets, and a typewriter, but if none of those are on hand, spare books and Broadway music can be easily substituted.

She prefers to be wild and free, though. Whether it includes adventuring through the Rocky Mountains or curled up at a local bookshop, she uses her freedom to produce art. From books to scarves to paintings, Ms. Seaver strives to honor her King in every aspect of her creative works. She desires her stories to hold a meaning beyond the tale and attempts to follow in the footsteps of storytellers who came before her.

You can find her and all of her wild adventures at ekseaver.wordpress.com or on Instagram @ekseaver.author